Text and illustrations © 2013 Bayard éditions

Published in North America in 2015 by Owlkids Books Inc.

Published in Quebec under the title *Ronchonette Cocolle* in 2013 by Bayard Jeunesse Canada.

Owlkids Books acknowledges the financial support of the Canada Council for the Arts, the Ontario Arts Council, the Government of Canada through the Canada Book Fund (CBF) and the Government of Ontario through the Ontario Media Development Corporation's Book Initiative for our publishing activities.

Published in Canada by   Published in the United States by
Owlkids Books Inc.   Owlkids Books Inc.
10 Lower Spadina Avenue   1700 Fourth Street
Toronto, ON M5V 2Z2   Berkeley, CA 94710

Library and Archives Canada Cataloguing in Publication

Delacroix, Sibylle
[Ronchonette cocolle. English]
       Prickly Jenny / written by Sibylle Delacroix ; translated by Karen Li.

Translation of: Ronchonette cocolle.
ISBN 978-1-77147-129-9 (bound)

       I. Li, Karen, translator II. Title. III. Title: Ronchonette cocolle. English.

PZ7.D4357Pr 2015   j843'.92   C2014-905133-6

Library of Congress Control Number: 2014947496

Manufactured in Dongguan, China, in September 2014, by Toppan Leefung Packaging & Printing (Dongguan) Co., Ltd.
Job #BAYDC10

A   B   C   D   E   F

Publisher of Chirp, chickaDEE and OWL
www.owlkidsbooks.com

Prickly Jenny

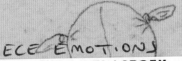

ECE EMOTIONS

Sibylle Delacroix

Owlkids Books

Jenny doesn't say good morning because, really, what's so good about it?

Jenny doesn't want her new
polka-dotted dress.

She wants to wear her old
T-shirt, and that's that.

Daddy takes her to the fair, but
Jenny grumbles and drags her feet.

There's nothing but ice cream for dessert, and Jenny says she wants nothing to do with it.

Jenny is tired, but nap time is
for babies.

Jenny says, "Leave me alone!" But she cries when Mommy goes away.

The only person who gets hugs from Jenny is Jojo the bunny.

Jenny is feeling out of sorts, but she doesn't want to talk about it. She just wants to be loved.

Jenny holds up her drawings, but she doesn't want to hear "wow" or "that's nice!"

Wait...Is that a smile, Jenny?

Oops—if you fuss about it, Jenny will go back to grumbling.

Jenny doesn't know what she wants today. But tomorrow, when she's bigger, it will get better.